BIGsteps
for Little Monsters

STORIES TO SHARE FOR EACH BIG STEP

By Sarah Albee • Illustrated by Tom Brannon

Dalmatian Press, LLC, 2005. All rights reserved.
Published by Dalmatian Press, LLC, 2005. The DALMATIAN PRESS name and logo
are trademarks of Dalmatian Press, LLC, Franklin, Tennessee 37067.
No part of this book may be reproduced or copied in any form
without written permission from the copyright owner.

Printed in China
ISBN: 1-40371-041-4 (X)   ISBN: 1-40371-272-7 (M)

05 06 07 08 SFO 10 9 8 7 6 5 4 3 2 1

My Baby Brother Is a Little Monster

"Hi, Henry," said Big Bird. "Ready to go to the park?"

"I'm ready," replied Henry. "But my mom can't take us until my brother wakes up from his nap."

"Oh, okay," said Big Bird.

Henry sighed. "We have to play inside until he's ready."

"Nice to see you, Big Bird," said Henry's mother. "Calvin should be awake soon."

Just then, Big Bird heard a horrible noise. "Wow! What's that?" he said.

Henry rolled his eyes. "That's my brother. He's awake."

"Big Bird," said Henry, "meet Calvin."
Big Bird smiled at Calvin.
Calvin drooled and blew bubbles.

"Can we go to the park now?" Henry asked.

"In a few mintues," said Henry's mother.

"Mom, come see the cool castle we made," Henry called.

Just at that moment, Calvin dumped a box of cereal all over the floor.

While his mother was cleaning up the cereal, Calvin crawled over and knocked down the castle.

"Gee," said Big Bird. "You want to play jacks or something?"

Henry shook his head sadly. "Nah, we can't. Calvin might try to put them in his mouth. You're not supposed to play with little toys when there's a baby around."

"Mom, *now* can we go to the park?" asked Henry.

"Pretty soon, honey," replied his mother. "Oh, isn't your brother adorable? Let me take a picture of the two of you together."

"Ouch!" said Henry.

"Why don't you tell him not to do that?" asked Big Bird.

"He doesn't understand that it hurts," replied Henry. "He's just a *little* monster."

"Eeeew! Mom!" called Henry, holding his nose.
"Calvin needs to be changed!"

Henry's mother carried Calvin away to change
his diaper.

"Mom, can we go to the park *now*?" Henry shouted over the noise Calvin was making.

"Soon, honey," his mother shouted back. "Calvin's hungry. I have to feed him. Then can we go."

"Your baby brother sure is loud!" yelled Big Bird.

"I wish you'd hurry up and eat that!" Henry told his brother.

SPLAT! Calvin decided he was finished with his lunch.

"Wow," said Big Bird. "Your baby brother sure is messy."

Henry had had enough. "I'm sick of having a baby around! He makes dumb baby noises and he messes up my toys and he throws food around. I wish," said Henry, his lip starting to tremble, "I wish I didn't have a baby brother!"

Henry's mother gave Henry a big hug. "Sweetie, I know it can be hard to have a little brother. It's okay to feel angry with him sometimes. Calvin is lucky to have such a patient big brother."

"Really?" said Henry, wiping his eyes.

"Come on! Let's go to the park!" said his mother.

A little while later, as they were playing catch, Big Bird stopped. "Hey, Henry," he said softly, "I think Calvin just said your name."

Henry hurried over to Calvin. "Mom!" he shrieked. "Hey, Mom! Calvin said my name!"

Henry's mother ran over to listen, too.

"En-wee, En-wee," Calvin said.

The End

ELMO'S

First Babysitter

Elmo is so excited! Elmo is going to have a babysitter tonight! Her name is Emily.

There's the doorbell! That must be Emily!

Um, wait a minute. Maybe Elmo doesn't really want a babysitter after all.

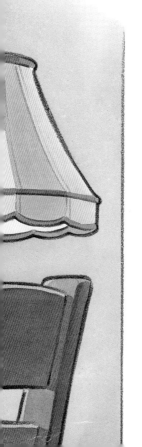

It *is* Emily. She looks nice, doesn't she? Elmo's mommy and daddy wrote down the phone number of the place they're going tonight. And they also wrote the phone numbers of our neighbors, just in case. Now it's time to hug Mommy and Daddy good-bye.

Restaurant
555-9423
Neighbors
555-9641
555-8003

Did you see what we made? Kooky faces! Elmo
made this one all by himself!

Wow! Elmo likes this music!

Elmo's toe feels all better now. And look—Emily brought bubbles for Elmo to play with in the bathtub. When Mommy and Daddy give Elmo a bath, Elmo never gets to blow bubbles.

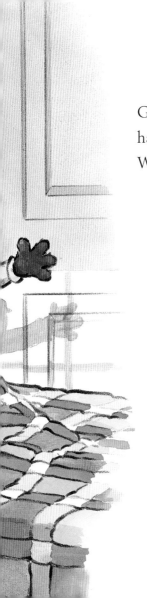

Good morning, Mommy!
Good morning, Daddy! Elmo liked
having a babysitter! It was fun!
When is Emily coming back?

The End

Elmo Goes
to the
Doctor

Elmo and his mommy were on their way to the doctor's office. "But, Mommy," Elmo said, "Elmo doesn't need to go to the doctor. Elmo feels just fine."

"It's time for your checkup, Elmo," said his mother.

"Is Elmo going to get . . . a shot?" Elmo asked in a small voice.

"Yes, Elmo," his mother replied.

"Maybe Elmo can ask Dr. Diane to give him some pink medicine to drink instead," Elmo whispered to himself.

The waiting room was crowded.

Elmo colored at a little table. "Elmo really feels fine, Mommy," he said. "Let's just go home."

RECEPTION

TAMMY

Just then, Rhonda, the nurse, came into the waiting room. "Elmo!" she called.

"Elmo doesn't need a shot today," Elmo said as he followed her into the examining room.

Rhonda smiled. "Let's start by measuring your height and weight," she said.

Rhonda tested Elmo's eyes.

She tested his ears.

She tested his blood pressure
by blowing up a cushion
around his arm.

Then Dr. Diane came in. She said hello to Elmo and his mother.

"Hi, Doctor," Elmo answered. "Elmo doesn't need to get a shot today. Elmo can just drink that pink medicine, OK?"

Dr. Diane shook her head. "Sorry, Elmo, but you do need a shot today. It will only hurt for a second. The medicine in the shot will help to keep you from getting sick."

"Oh," said Elmo.

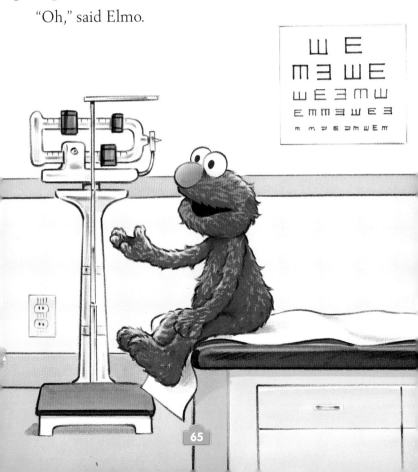

Dr. Diane asked Elmo a lot of questions.

"Do you wear a bike helmet? Do you ride in a car seat? Do you make sure a grown-up is right there watching when you go swimming?"

"Yes," Elmo answered to each question.

Then Dr. Diane tapped Elmo's knees with a little hammer until they jumped.

She looked inside his ears with a special light.
Then she looked inside his mouth.

Then Elmo lay on his back and Dr. Diane felt
his tummy.

She listened carefully to his back while Elmo took deep breaths. Then she listened to his heart.

Finally, Elmo bent over so the doctor could look at his back.

"Well, Elmo, you are a healthy little monster," said Dr. Diane.

"Oh, good," said Elmo. "Time to go, right?"

"Not just yet, Elmo," said Dr. Diane. "Rhonda has to give you a shot now. I know you're a little scared, but you know what? It's OK. When I was your age, I was scared of shots, too."

The shot hurt, but just for a second. "Is that it?" asked Elmo, opening his eyes.

"That's it, Elmo!" said Dr. Diane. "You can go get a sticker now."

"Wow!" said Elmo, hopping down from the table. "That wasn't so bad!"

A few days later, Elmo had a tummy ache.
Elmo's mommy called the doctor.

"We're going to Dr. Diane's office in a little
while," she said.

Elmo's tummy hurt even more.

This time, Elmo didn't feel like doing any
drawing in the waiting room.

When Elmo's name was called, he and his mommy
went into the examining room.

"Hello, Elmo," said Dr. Diane. She began to touch
his tummy very gently. "Where does it hurt?" she asked.

"All over," Elmo answered.

"What did you have for breakfast this morning?"
asked Dr. Diane, still pressing gently on his tummy.

"Elmo ate all the monstermallows out of the Monster Flakes cereal box," Elmo said.

"Aha," said Dr. Diane. "I think the reason your tummy hurts is that you overdid it a little. I'm pretty sure you'll be feeling better soon." She helped him to sit up. "You can go home now, Elmo," she said.

"You mean Elmo doesn't have to get a shot today?" asked Elmo.

"No, Elmo," replied Dr. Diane. "You don't get a shot every time you come to the doctor."

"Thanks, Dr. Diane!" said Elmo. "Elmo feels better already!"

The End